5-2014 MidAmerica 1695

IDW STAR TREK®

JOHNSON
MOLNAR

GO BOLDLY

ENLIST IN STARFLEET

WRITER
MIKE JOHNSON

ARTIST
STEPHEN MOLNAR AND JOE PHILLIPS

COLORIST
JOHN RAUCH

LETTERER
NEIL UYETAKE

BASED ON THE ORIGINAL TELEPLAY OF *THE GALILEO SEVEN* BY
SAMUEL A. PEEPLES AND SHIMON WINCELBERG

CREATIVE CONSULTANT
ROBERTO ORCI

EDITOR
SCOTT DUNBIER

Spotlight

Visit us at www.abdopublishing.com

Reinforced library bound editions published in 2014 by Spotlight, a division of the ABDO Group, PO Box 398166, Minneapolis, MN 55439. Spotlight produces high-quality reinforced library bound editions for schools and libraries. Published by agreement with IDW.

Printed in the United States of America, North Mankato, Minnesota.
042013
092013
This book contains at least 10% recycled material.

STAR TREK created by Gene Roddenberry.
Special thanks to Risa Kessler and John Van Citters of CBS Consumer Products for their invaluable assistance.

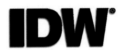

Library of Congress Cataloging-in-Publication Data

Johnson, Mike.
The Galileo Seven / story by Mike Johnson ; art by Stephen Molnar.
volumes cm. -- (Star Trek)
ISBN 978-1-61479-159-1 (part 1) -- ISBN 978-1-61479-160-7 (part 2)
1. Graphic novels. I. Molnar, Stephen, illustrator. II. Title.
PZ7.7.J6417Gal 2014
741.5'973--dc23
2013004266

All Spotlight books are reinforced library bindings and manufactured in the United States of America.

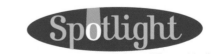

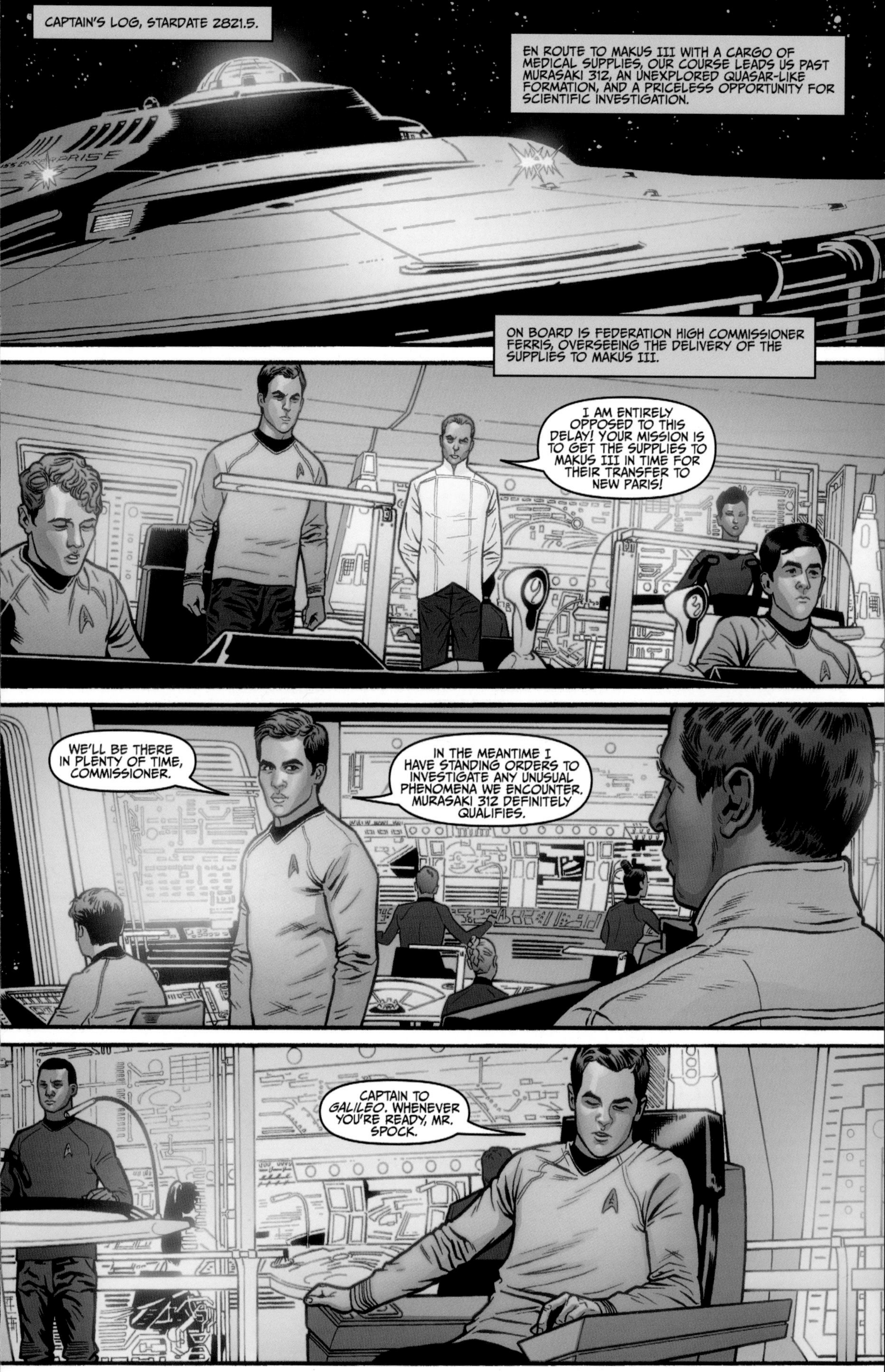

CAPTAIN'S LOG, STARDATE 2821.5.
EN ROUTE TO MAKUS III WITH A CARGO OF MEDICAL SUPPLIES, OUR COURSE LEADS US PAST MURASAKI 312, AN UNEXPLORED QUASAR-LIKE FORMATION, AND A PRICELESS OPPORTUNITY FOR SCIENTIFIC INVESTIGATION.
ON BOARD IS FEDERATION HIGH COMMISSIONER FERRIS, OVERSEEING THE DELIVERY OF THE SUPPLIES TO MAKUS III.
I AM ENTIRELY OPPOSED TO THIS DELAY! YOUR MISSION IS TO GET THE SUPPLIES TO MAKUS III IN TIME FOR THEIR TRANSFER TO NEW PARIS!
WE'LL BE THERE IN PLENTY OF TIME, COMMISSIONER.
IN THE MEANTIME I HAVE STANDING ORDERS TO INVESTIGATE ANY UNUSUAL PHENOMENA WE ENCOUNTER. MURASAKI 312 DEFINITELY QUALIFIES.
CAPTAIN TO GALILEO. WHENEVER YOU'RE READY, MR. SPOCK.

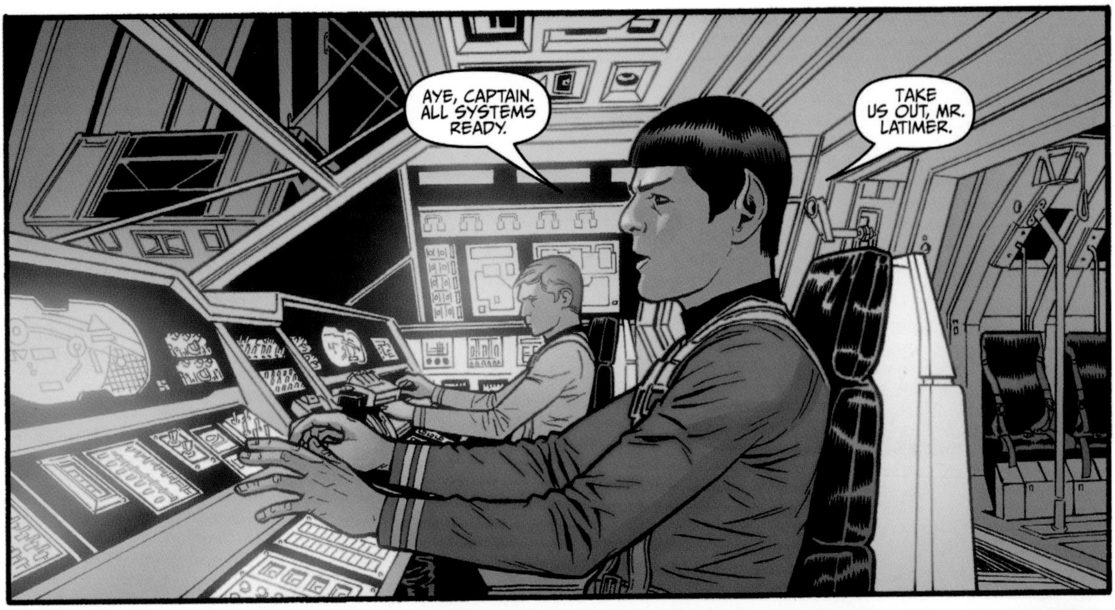
AYE, CAPTAIN. ALL SYSTEMS READY.
TAKE US OUT, MR. LATIMER.

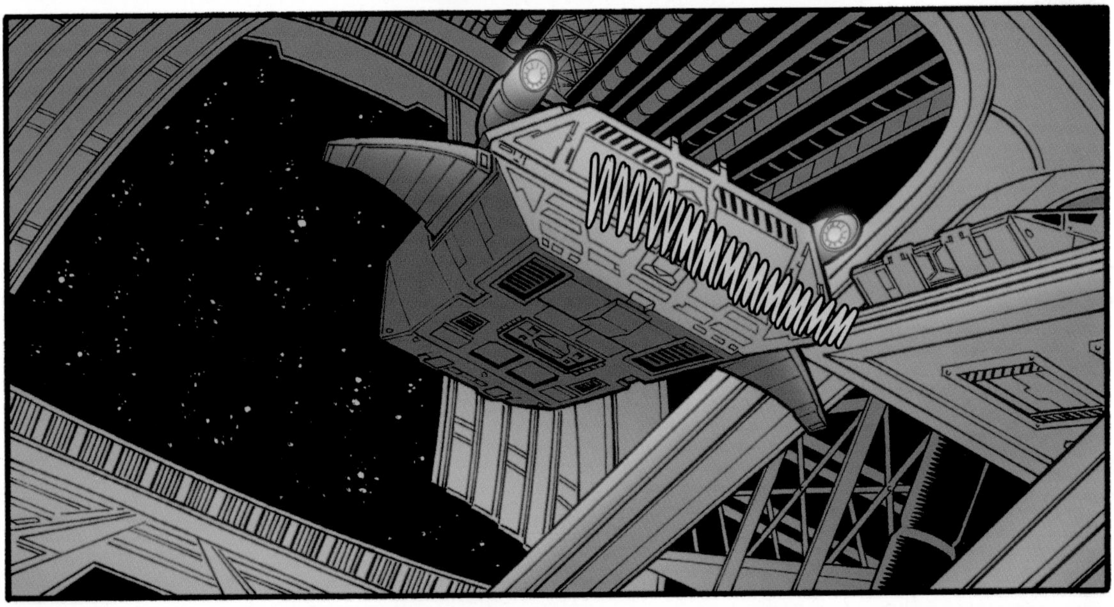
WWWMMMMMMMMMMMM

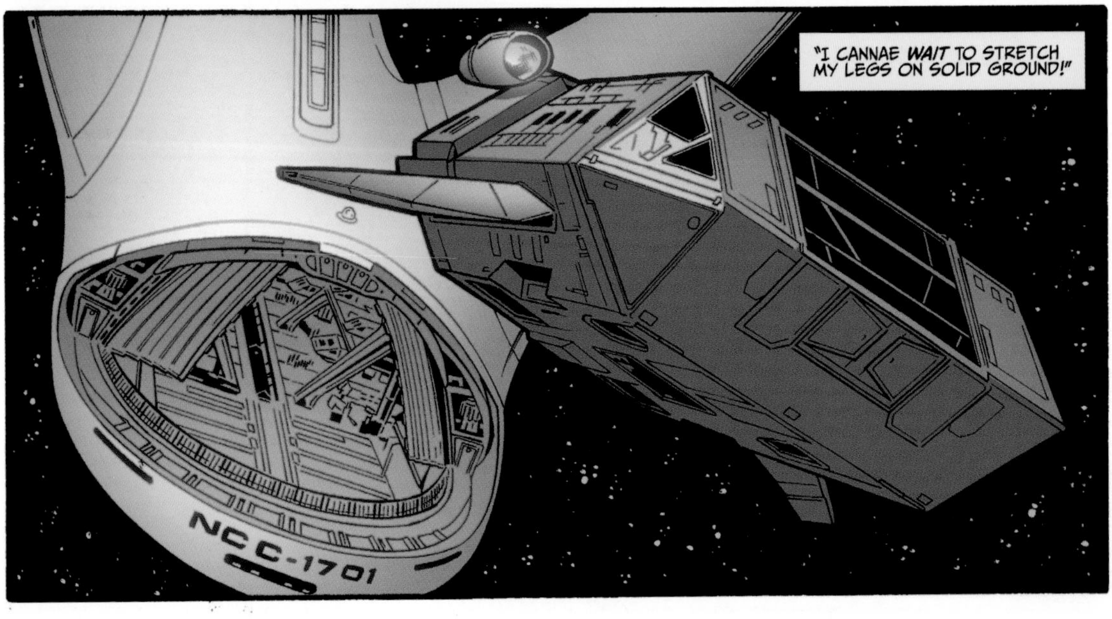
"I CANNAE *WAIT* TO STRETCH MY LEGS ON SOLID GROUND!"
NCC-1701

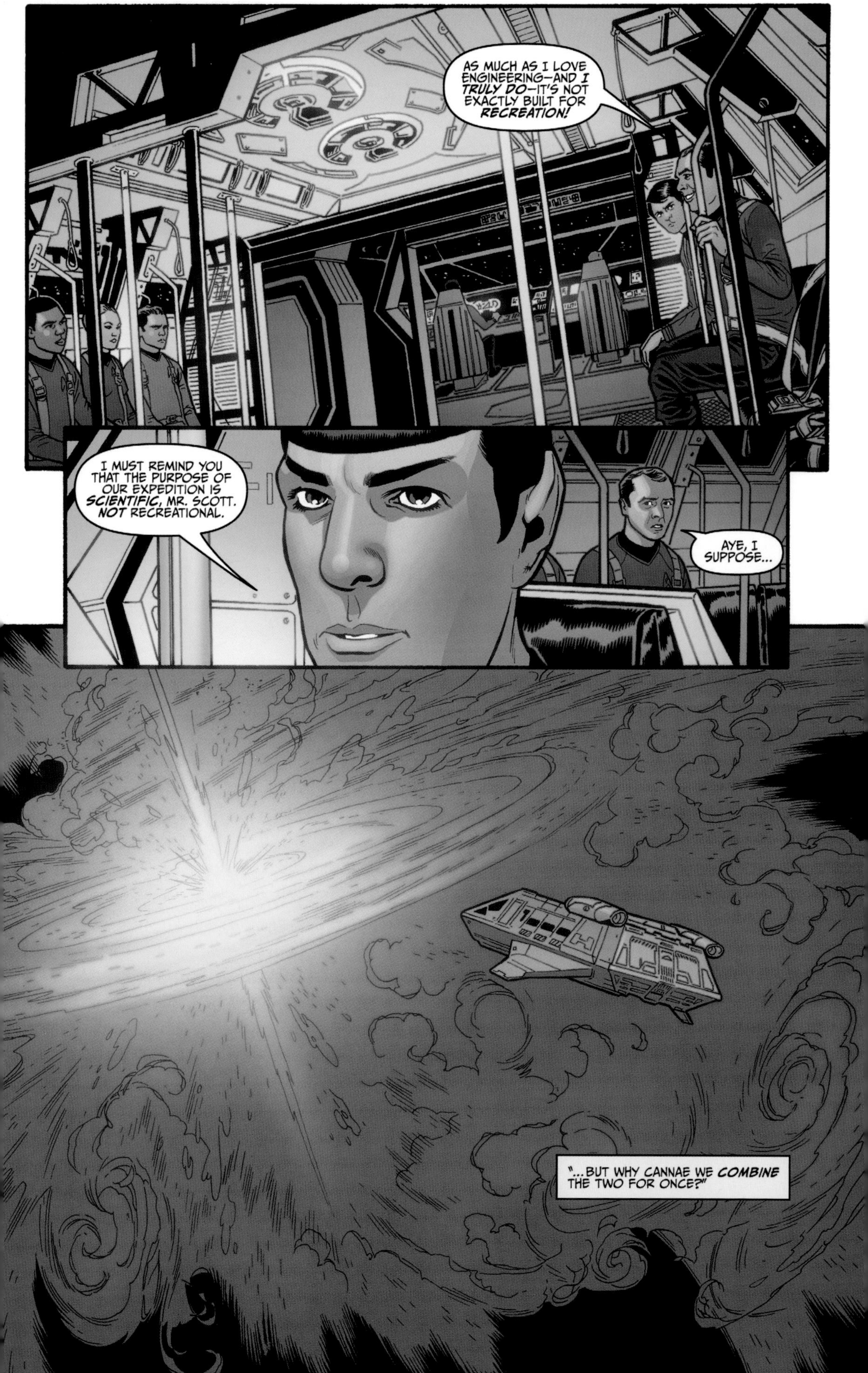
AS MUCH AS I LOVE ENGINEERING—AND I TRULY DO—IT'S NOT EXACTLY BUILT FOR RECREATION!
I MUST REMIND YOU THAT THE PURPOSE OF OUR EXPEDITION IS SCIENTIFIC, MR. SCOTT. NOT RECREATIONAL.
AYE, I SUPPOSE...
"...BUT WHY CANNAE WE COMBINE THE TWO FOR ONCE?"

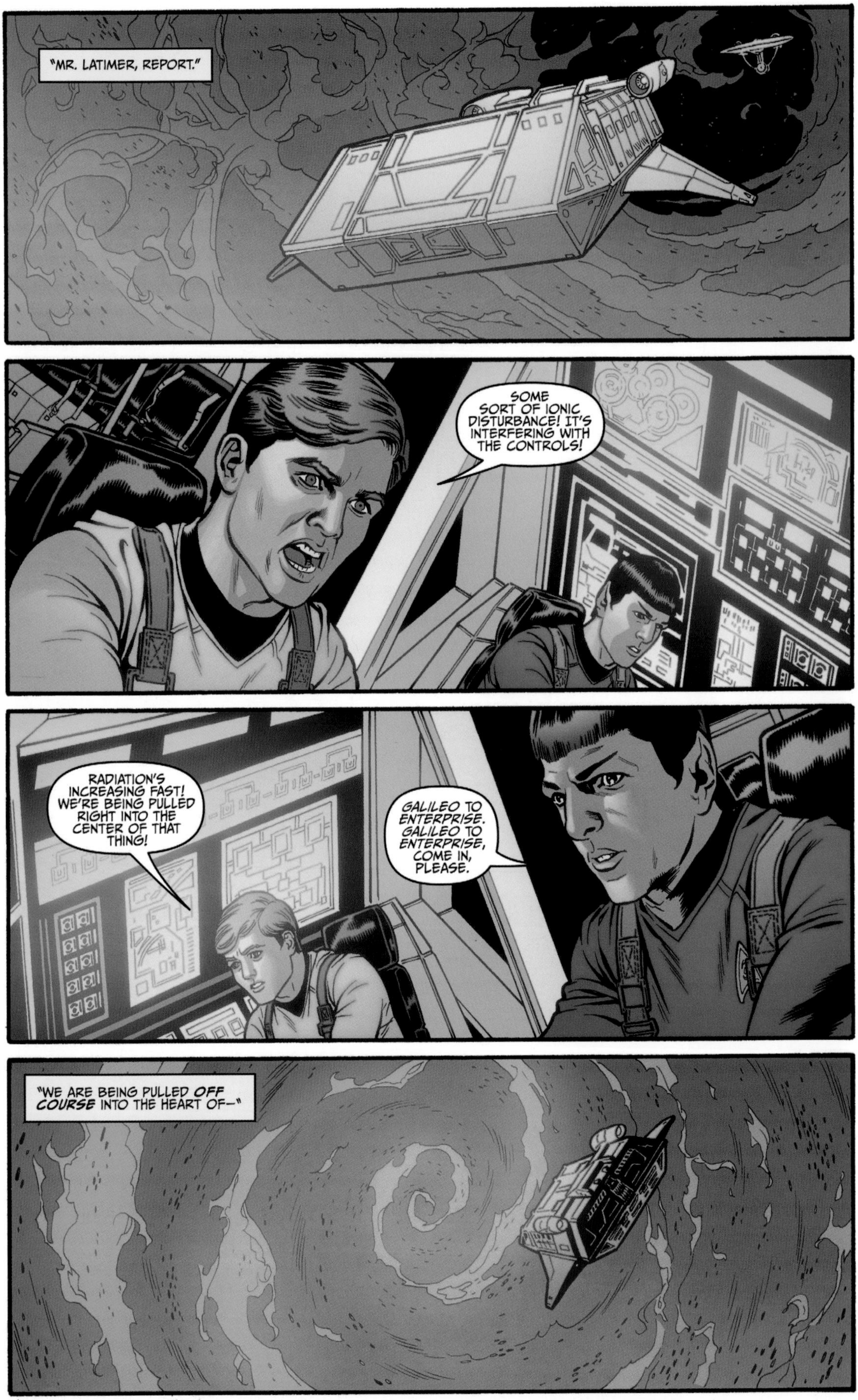
"MR. LATIMER, REPORT."
SOME SORT OF IONIC DISTURBANCE! IT'S INTERFERING WITH THE CONTROLS!
RADIATION'S INCREASING FAST! WE'RE BEING PULLED RIGHT INTO THE CENTER OF THAT THING!
GALILEO TO *ENTERPRISE*. *GALILEO* TO *ENTERPRISE*, COME IN, PLEASE.
"WE ARE BEING PULLED *OFF COURSE* INTO THE HEART OF--"

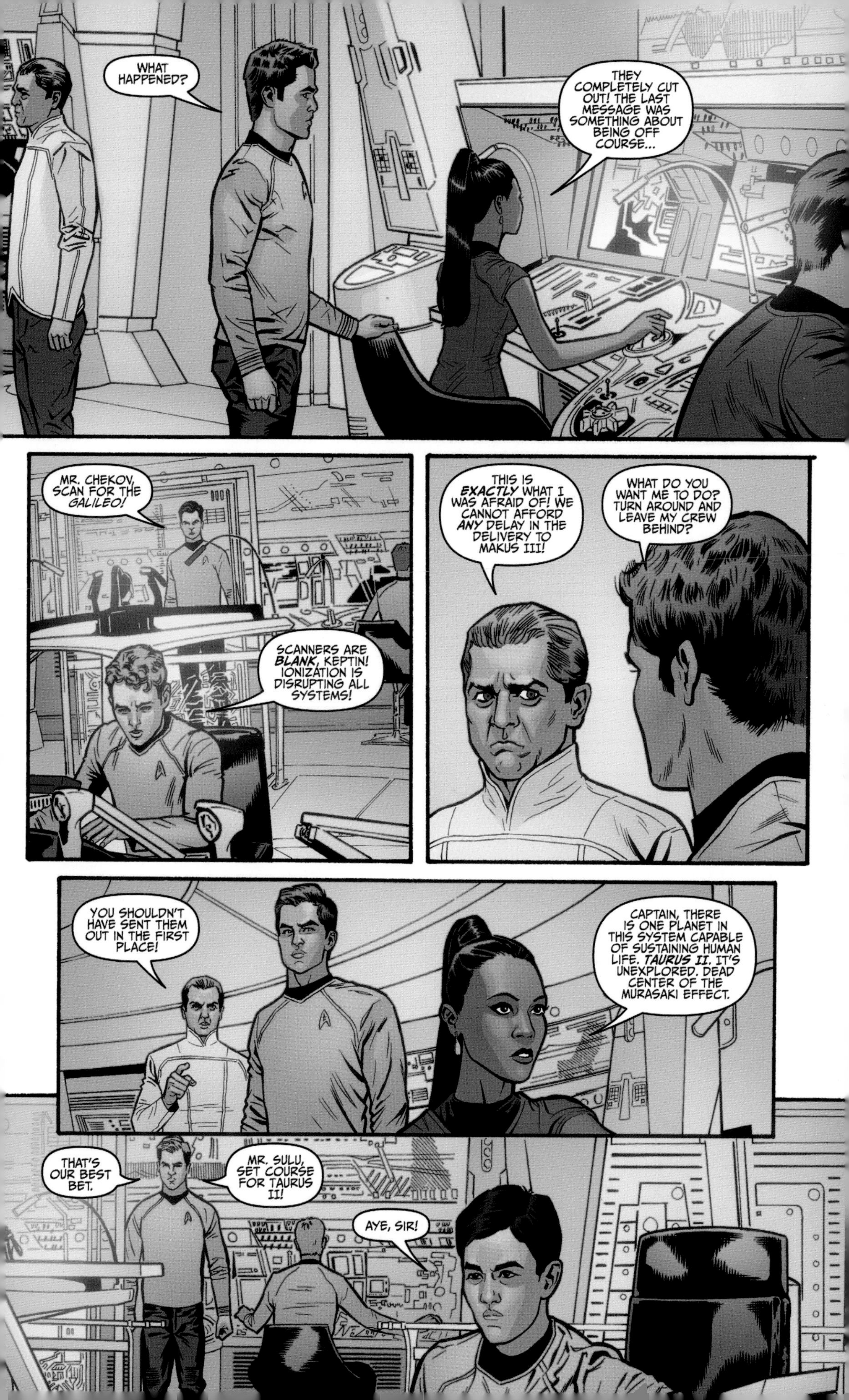
WHAT HAPPENED?
THEY COMPLETELY CUT OUT! THE LAST MESSAGE WAS SOMETHING ABOUT BEING OFF COURSE...
MR. CHEKOV, SCAN FOR THE *GALILEO!*
SCANNERS ARE **BLANK**, KEPTIN! IONIZATION IS DISRUPTING ALL SYSTEMS!
THIS IS ***EXACTLY*** WHAT I WAS AFRAID OF! WE CANNOT AFFORD ***ANY*** DELAY IN THE DELIVERY TO MAKUS III!
WHAT DO YOU WANT ME TO DO? TURN AROUND AND LEAVE MY CREW BEHIND?
YOU SHOULDN'T HAVE SENT THEM OUT IN THE FIRST PLACE!
CAPTAIN, THERE IS ONE PLANET IN THIS SYSTEM CAPABLE OF SUSTAINING HUMAN LIFE. ***TAURUS II***. IT'S UNEXPLORED. DEAD CENTER OF THE MURASAKI EFFECT.
THAT'S OUR BEST BET.
MR. SULU, SET COURSE FOR TAURUS II!
AYE, SIR!

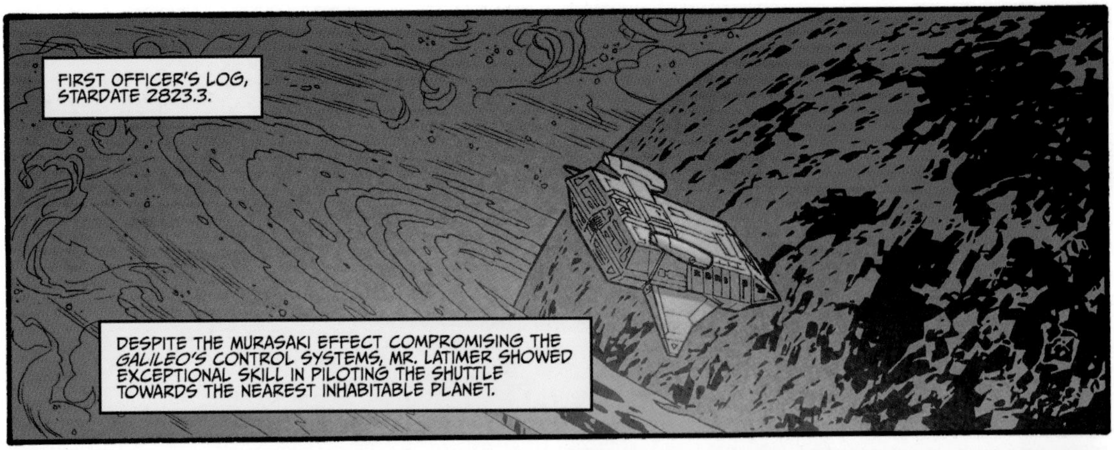
FIRST OFFICER'S LOG, STARDATE 2823.3.
DESPITE THE MURASAKI EFFECT COMPROMISING THE *GALILEO'S* CONTROL SYSTEMS, MR. LATIMER SHOWED EXCEPTIONAL SKILL IN PILOTING THE SHUTTLE TOWARDS THE NEAREST INHABITABLE PLANET.

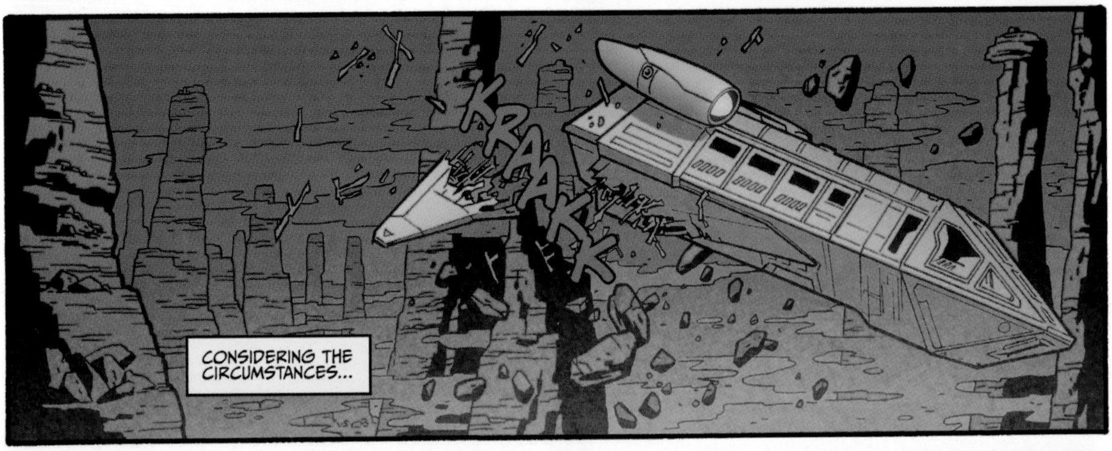
KRAAKK
CONSIDERING THE CIRCUMSTANCES...

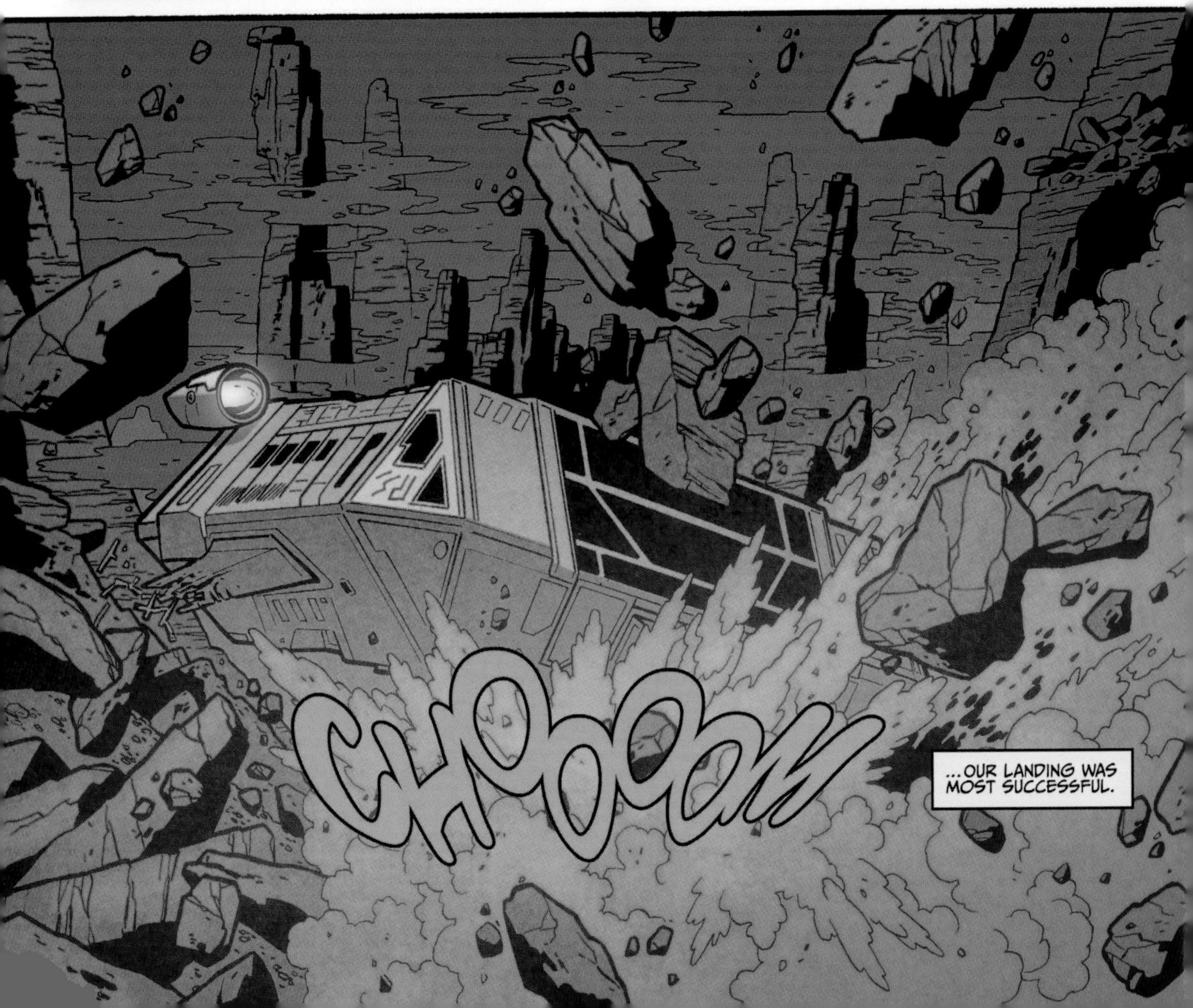
CHOOOOM
...OUR LANDING WAS MOST SUCCESSFUL.

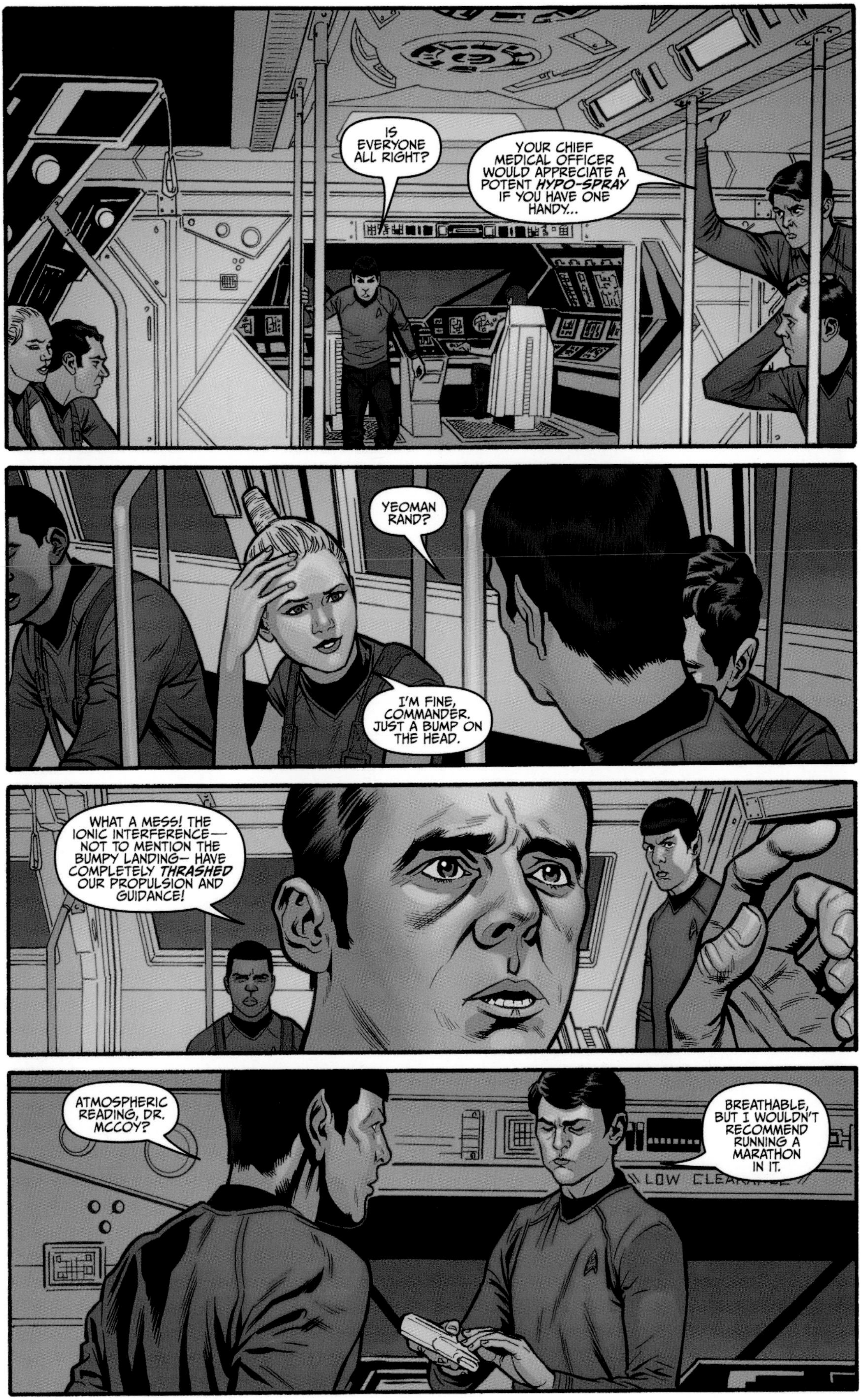
IS EVERYONE ALL RIGHT?
YOUR CHIEF MEDICAL OFFICER WOULD APPRECIATE A POTENT HYPO-SPRAY IF YOU HAVE ONE HANDY...
YEOMAN RAND?
I'M FINE, COMMANDER. JUST A BUMP ON THE HEAD.
WHAT A MESS! THE IONIC INTERFERENCE— NOT TO MENTION THE BUMPY LANDING— HAVE COMPLETELY THRASHED OUR PROPULSION AND GUIDANCE!
ATMOSPHERIC READING, DR. MCCOY?
BREATHABLE, BUT I WOULDN'T RECOMMEND RUNNING A MARATHON IN IT.

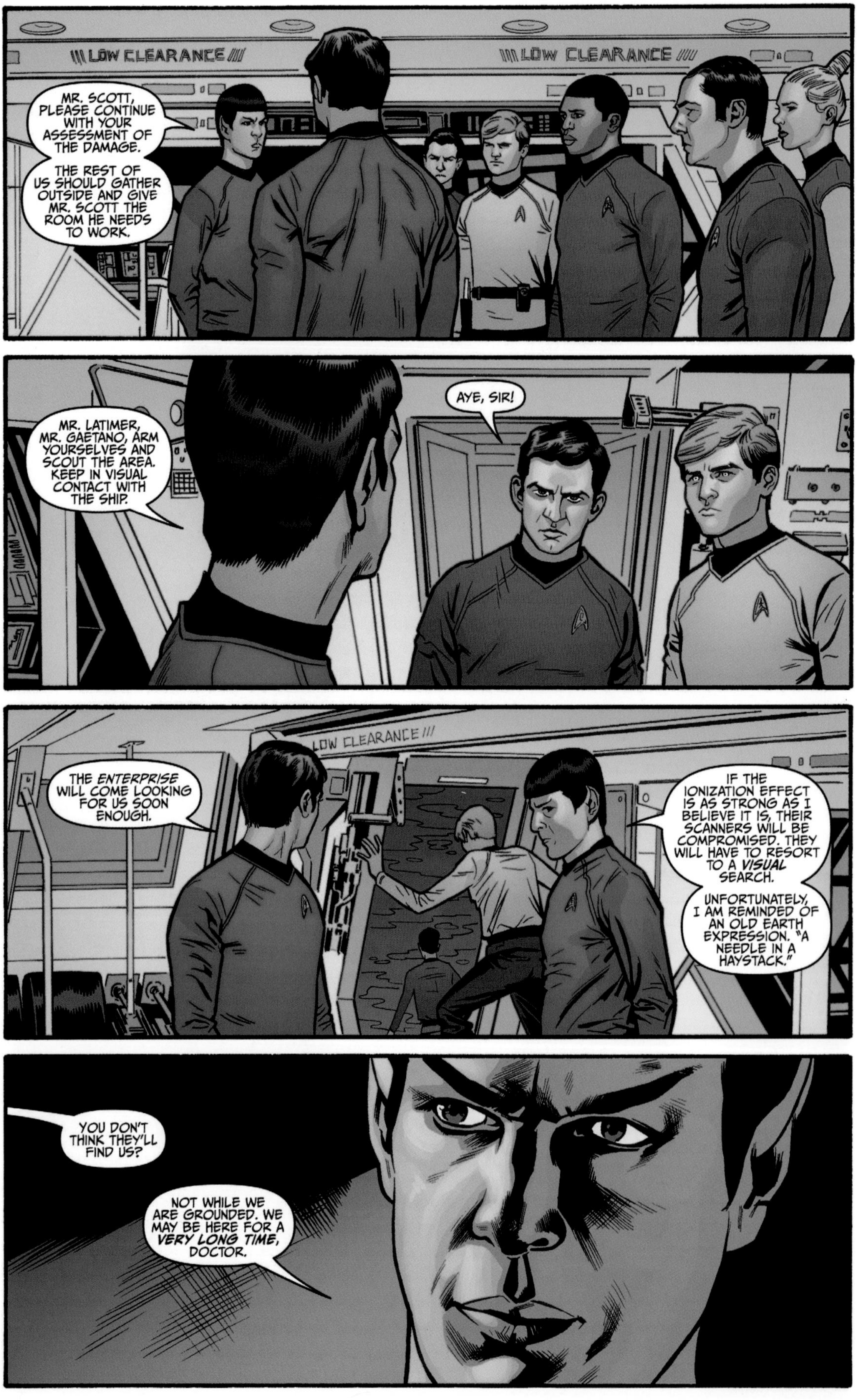
LOW CLEARANCE
LOW CLEARANCE
MR. SCOTT, PLEASE CONTINUE WITH YOUR ASSESSMENT OF THE DAMAGE.
THE REST OF US SHOULD GATHER OUTSIDE AND GIVE MR. SCOTT THE ROOM HE NEEDS TO WORK.
MR. LATIMER, MR. GAETANO, ARM YOURSELVES AND SCOUT THE AREA. KEEP IN VISUAL CONTACT WITH THE SHIP.
AYE, SIR!
LOW CLEARANCE
THE *ENTERPRISE* WILL COME LOOKING FOR US SOON ENOUGH.
IF THE IONIZATION EFFECT IS AS STRONG AS I BELIEVE IT IS, THEIR SCANNERS WILL BE COMPROMISED. THEY WILL HAVE TO RESORT TO A *VISUAL* SEARCH.
UNFORTUNATELY, I AM REMINDED OF AN OLD EARTH EXPRESSION. "A NEEDLE IN A HAYSTACK."
YOU DON'T THINK THEY'LL FIND US?
NOT WHILE WE ARE GROUNDED. WE MAY BE HERE FOR A ***VERY LONG TIME***, DOCTOR.

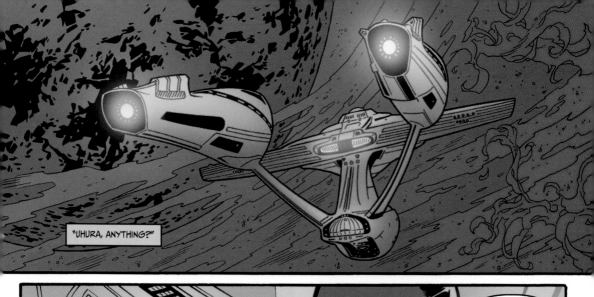

"UHURA, ANYTHING?"

NOTHING, CAPTAIN. THE QUASAR IS DISRUPTING ALL COMMUNICATIONS.

SPOCK... IF YOU CAN HEAR ME... I'M GOING TO KILL YOU IF YOU DON'T COME BACK...

KEPTIN, TRANSPORTERS ARE COMPROMISED BY THE IONIZATION! EVEN IF WE COULD FIND ZEM, WE COULD NOT BEAM ZEM BACK ABOARD!

KIRK TO SHUTTLE BAY.

PREPARE ALL SHUTTLES FOR IMMEDIATE DEPARTURE TO THE SURFACE OF TAURUS II FOR VISUAL RECONNAISSANCE. CORRELATE COORDINATES WITH MR. CHEKOV.

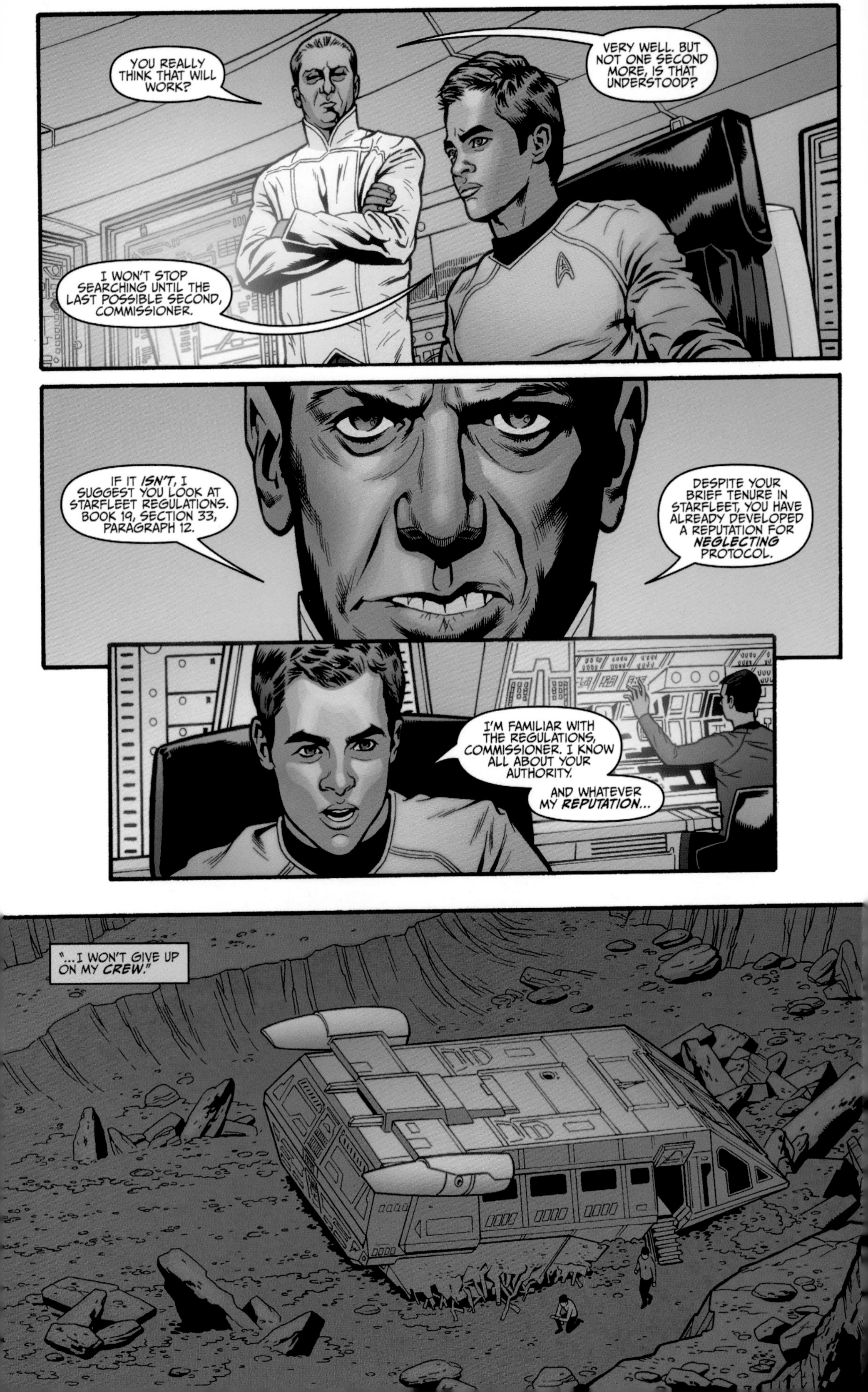
YOU REALLY THINK THAT WILL WORK?
VERY WELL. BUT NOT ONE SECOND MORE, IS THAT UNDERSTOOD?
I WON'T STOP SEARCHING UNTIL THE LAST POSSIBLE SECOND, COMMISSIONER.
IF IT *ISN'T*, I SUGGEST YOU LOOK AT STARFLEET REGULATIONS. BOOK 19, SECTION 33, PARAGRAPH 12.
DESPITE YOUR BRIEF TENURE IN STARFLEET, YOU HAVE ALREADY DEVELOPED A REPUTATION FOR ***NEGLECTING*** PROTOCOL.
I'M FAMILIAR WITH THE REGULATIONS, COMMISSIONER. I KNOW ALL ABOUT YOUR AUTHORITY.
AND WHATEVER MY ***REPUTATION***...
"...I WON'T GIVE UP ON MY ***CREW***."

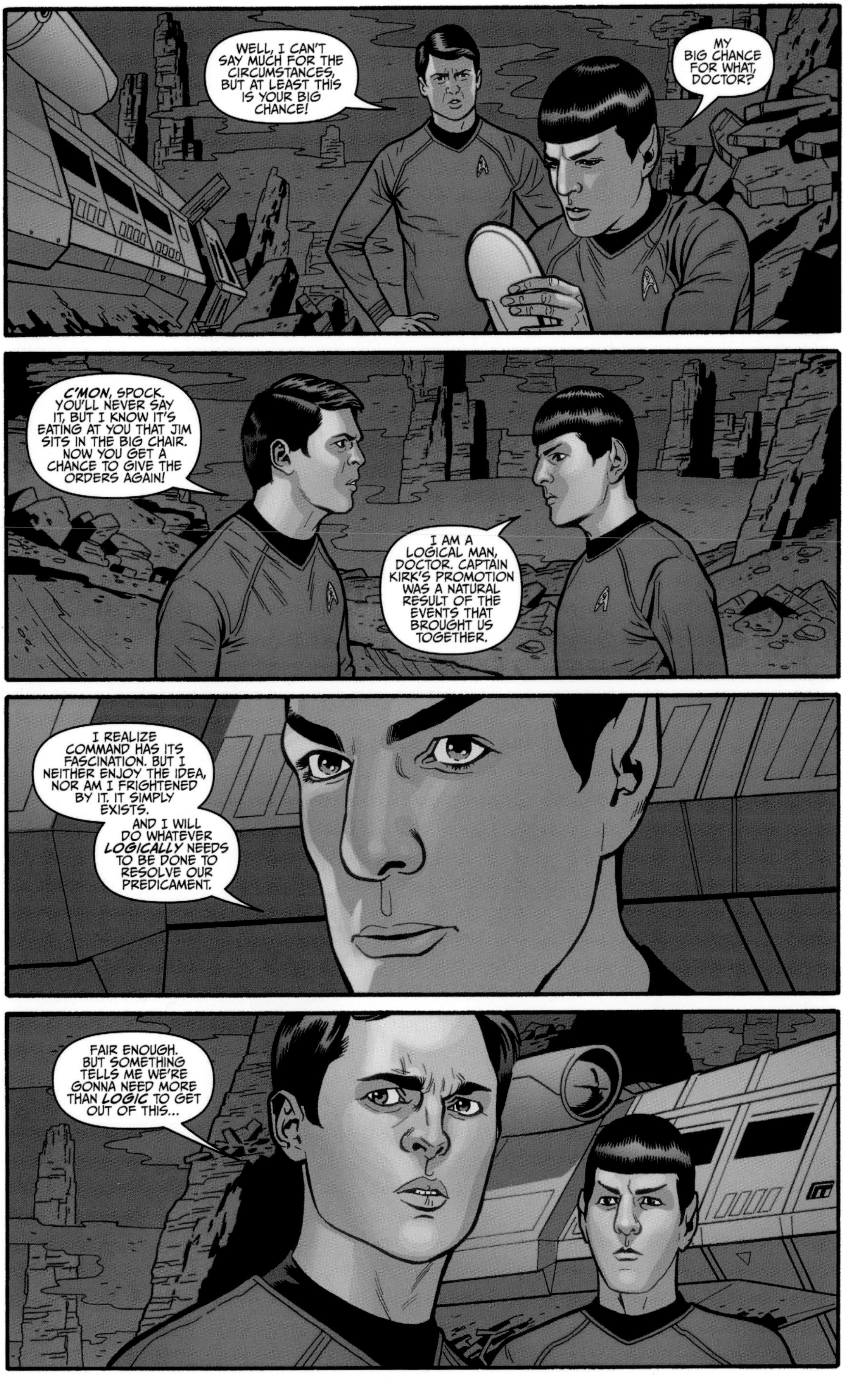
WELL, I CAN'T SAY MUCH FOR THE CIRCUMSTANCES, BUT AT LEAST THIS IS YOUR BIG CHANCE!
MY BIG CHANCE FOR WHAT, DOCTOR?
C'MON, SPOCK. YOU'LL NEVER SAY IT, BUT I KNOW IT'S EATING AT YOU THAT JIM SITS IN THE BIG CHAIR. NOW YOU GET A CHANCE TO GIVE THE ORDERS AGAIN!
I AM A LOGICAL MAN, DOCTOR. CAPTAIN KIRK'S PROMOTION WAS A NATURAL RESULT OF THE EVENTS THAT BROUGHT US TOGETHER.
I REALIZE COMMAND HAS ITS FASCINATION. BUT I NEITHER ENJOY THE IDEA, NOR AM I FRIGHTENED BY IT. IT SIMPLY EXISTS.
AND I WILL DO WHATEVER LOGICALLY NEEDS TO BE DONE TO RESOLVE OUR PREDICAMENT.
FAIR ENOUGH. BUT SOMETHING TELLS ME WE'RE GONNA NEED MORE THAN LOGIC TO GET OUT OF THIS...

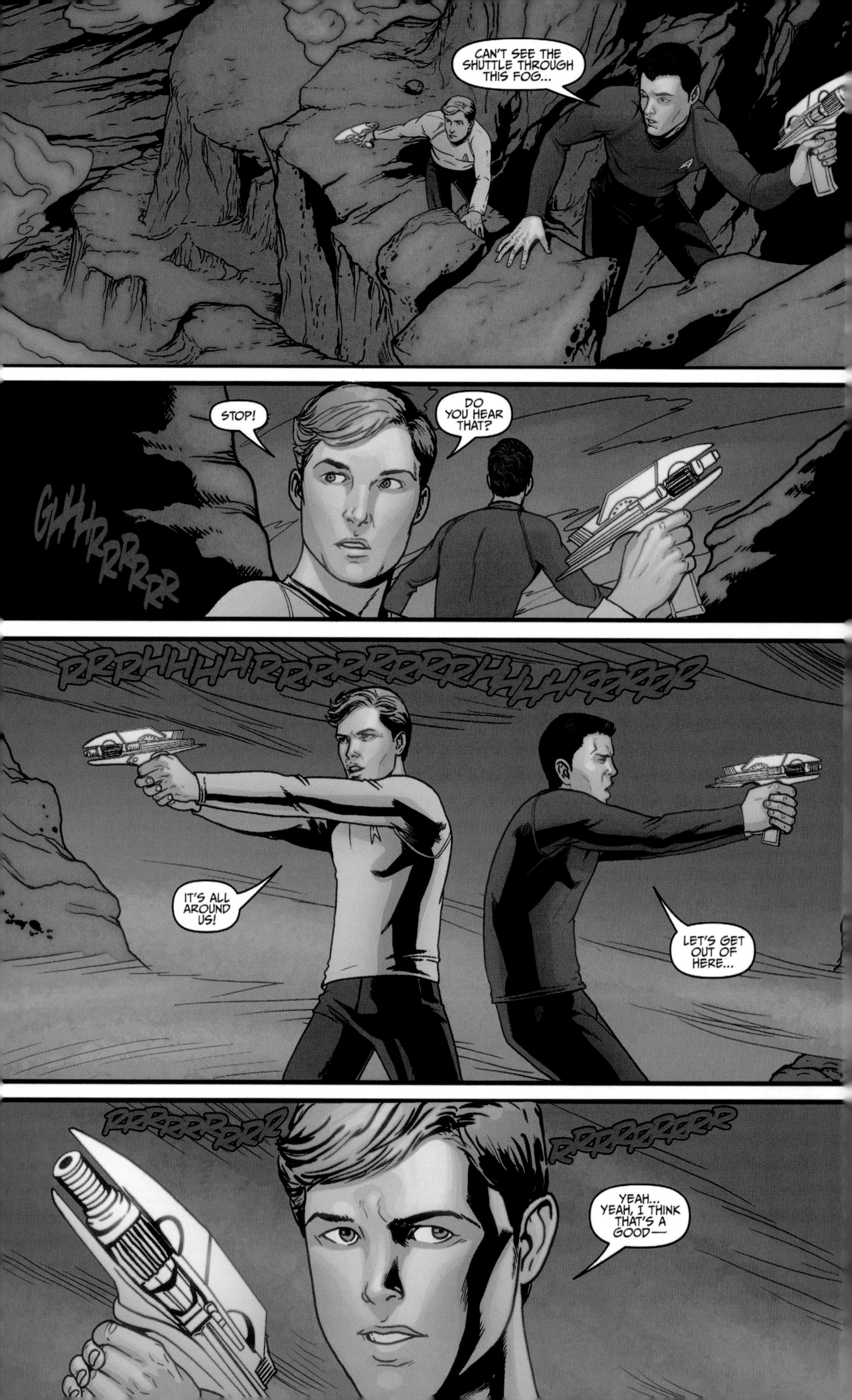
CAN'T SEE THE SHUTTLE THROUGH THIS FOG...
STOP!
DO YOU HEAR THAT?
GHHRRRRRR
RRRHHHRRRRRRRRRHHHRRRRR
IT'S ALL AROUND US!
LET'S GET OUT OF HERE...
RRRRRRRRR
RRRRRRRRR
YEAH... YEAH, I THINK THAT'S A GOOD—

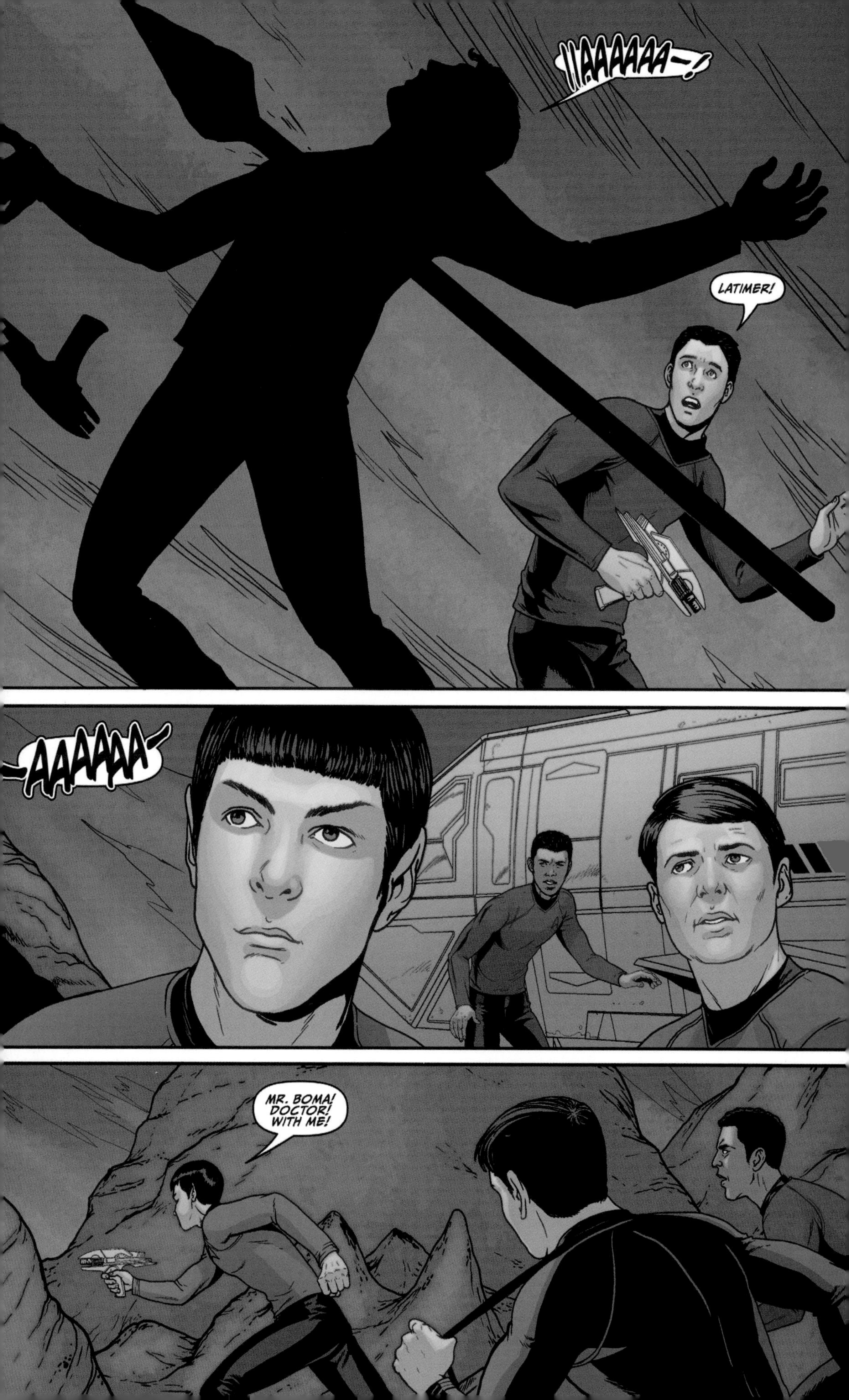
IIAAAAAA—!
LATIMER!
—AAAAAA—
MR. BOMA! DOCTOR! WITH ME!

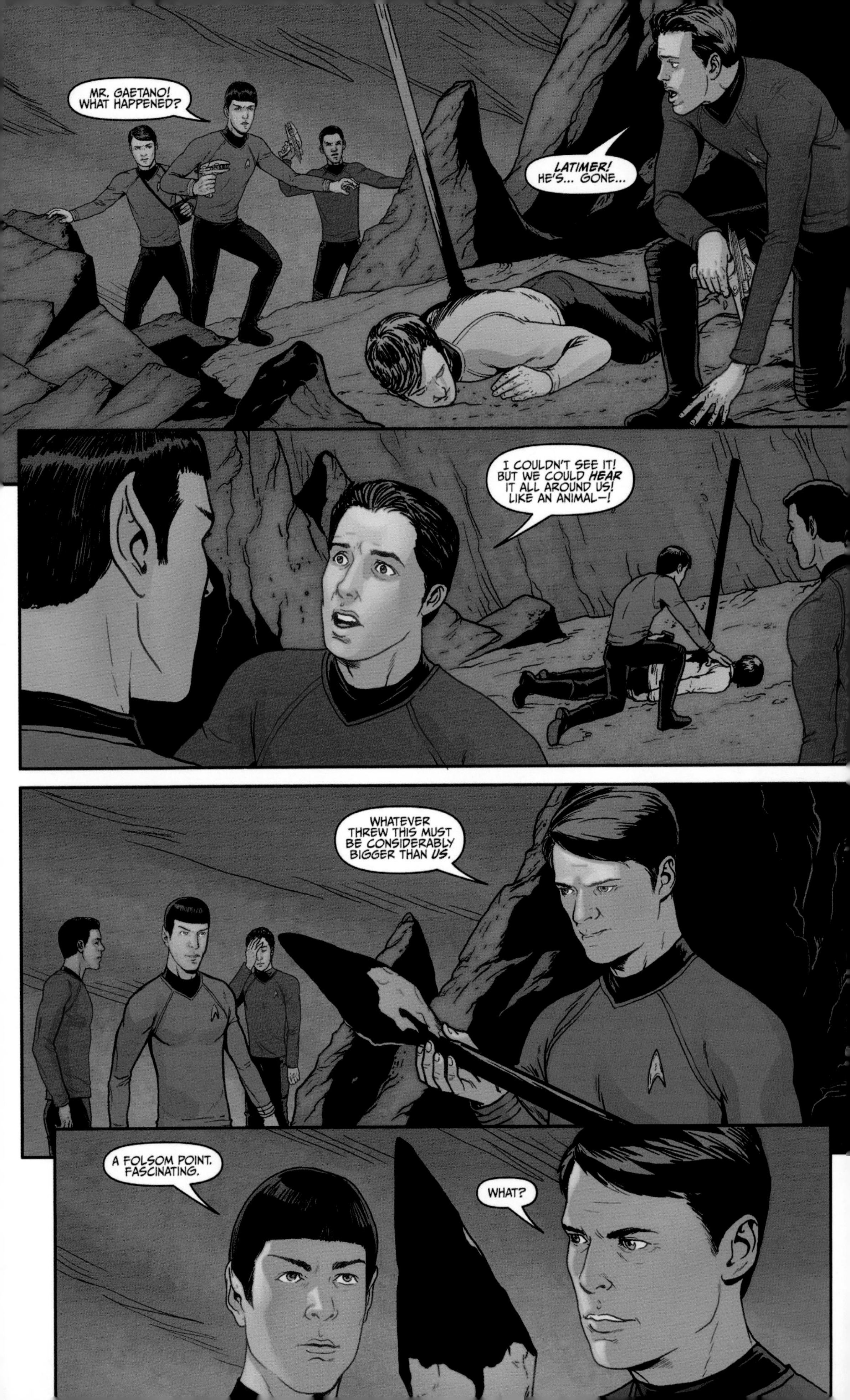
MR. GAETANO! WHAT HAPPENED?
LATIMER! HE'S... GONE...
I COULDN'T SEE IT! BUT WE COULD HEAR IT ALL AROUND US! LIKE AN ANIMAL—!
WHATEVER THREW THIS MUST BE CONSIDERABLY BIGGER THAN US.
A FOLSOM POINT. FASCINATING.
WHAT?

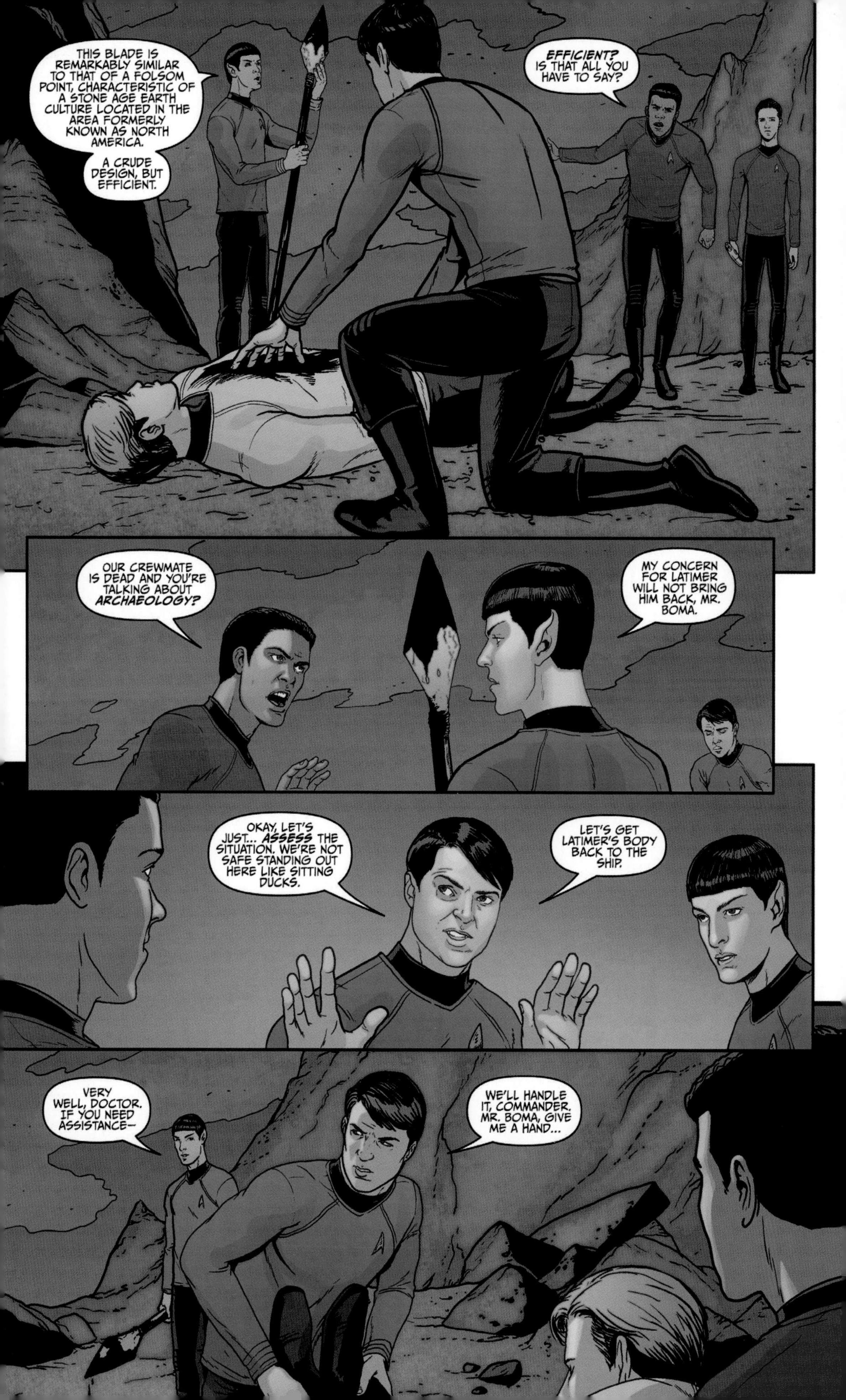
THIS BLADE IS REMARKABLY SIMILAR TO THAT OF A FOLSOM POINT, CHARACTERISTIC OF A STONE AGE EARTH CULTURE LOCATED IN THE AREA FORMERLY KNOWN AS NORTH AMERICA.
A CRUDE DESIGN, BUT EFFICIENT.
EFFICIENT? IS THAT ALL YOU HAVE TO SAY?
OUR CREWMATE IS DEAD AND YOU'RE TALKING ABOUT ARCHAEOLOGY?
MY CONCERN FOR LATIMER WILL NOT BRING HIM BACK, MR. BOMA.
OKAY, LET'S JUST... ASSESS THE SITUATION. WE'RE NOT SAFE STANDING OUT HERE LIKE SITTING DUCKS.
LET'S GET LATIMER'S BODY BACK TO THE SHIP.
VERY WELL, DOCTOR. IF YOU NEED ASSISTANCE—
WE'LL HANDLE IT, COMMANDER. MR. BOMA, GIVE ME A HAND...

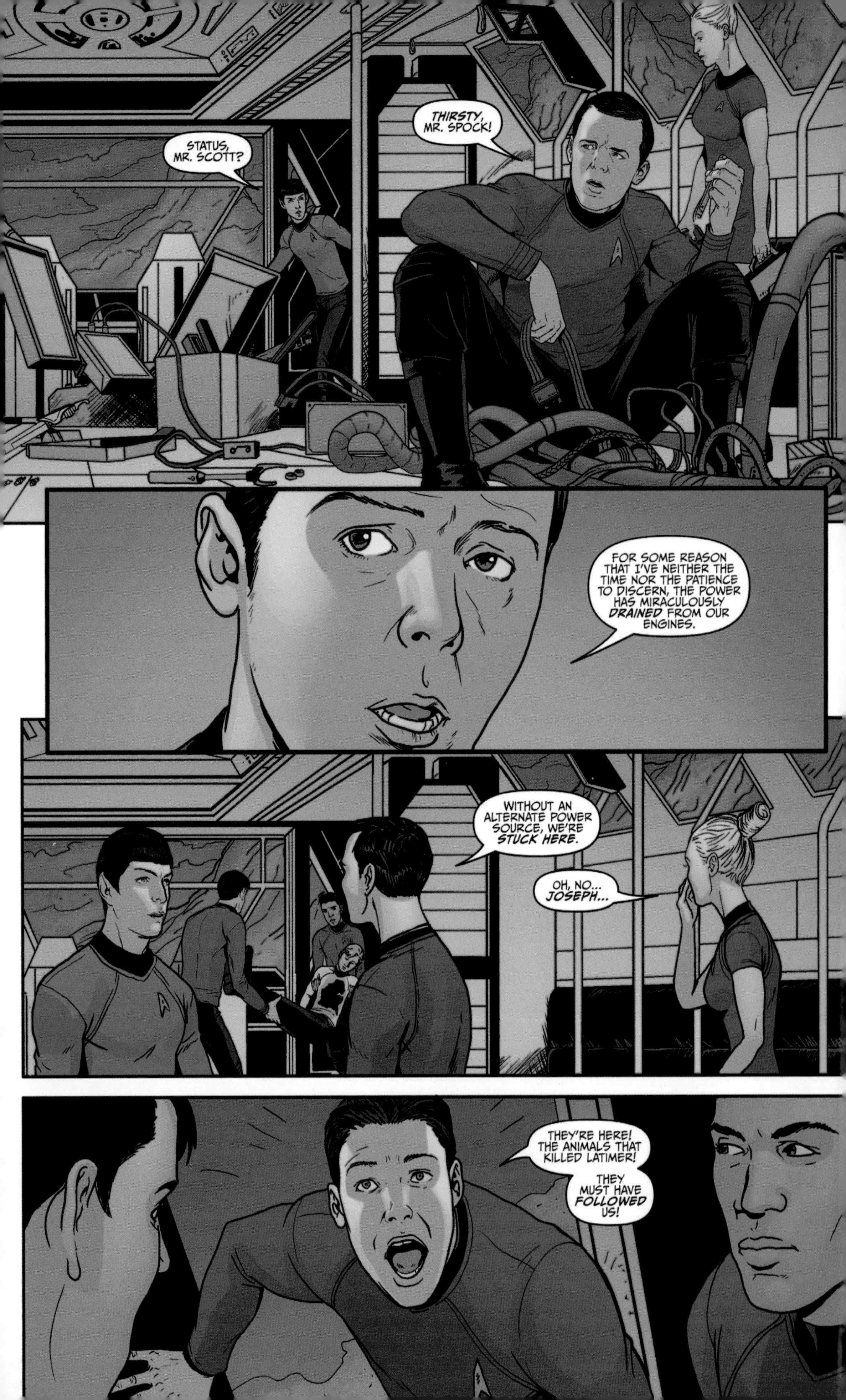
STATUS, MR. SCOTT?
THIRSTY, MR. SPOCK!
FOR SOME REASON THAT I'VE NEITHER THE TIME NOR THE PATIENCE TO DISCERN, THE POWER HAS MIRACULOUSLY DRAINED FROM OUR ENGINES.
WITHOUT AN ALTERNATE POWER SOURCE, WE'RE STUCK HERE.
OH, NO... JOSEPH...
THEY'RE HERE! THE ANIMALS THAT KILLED LATIMER!
THEY MUST HAVE FOLLOWED US!

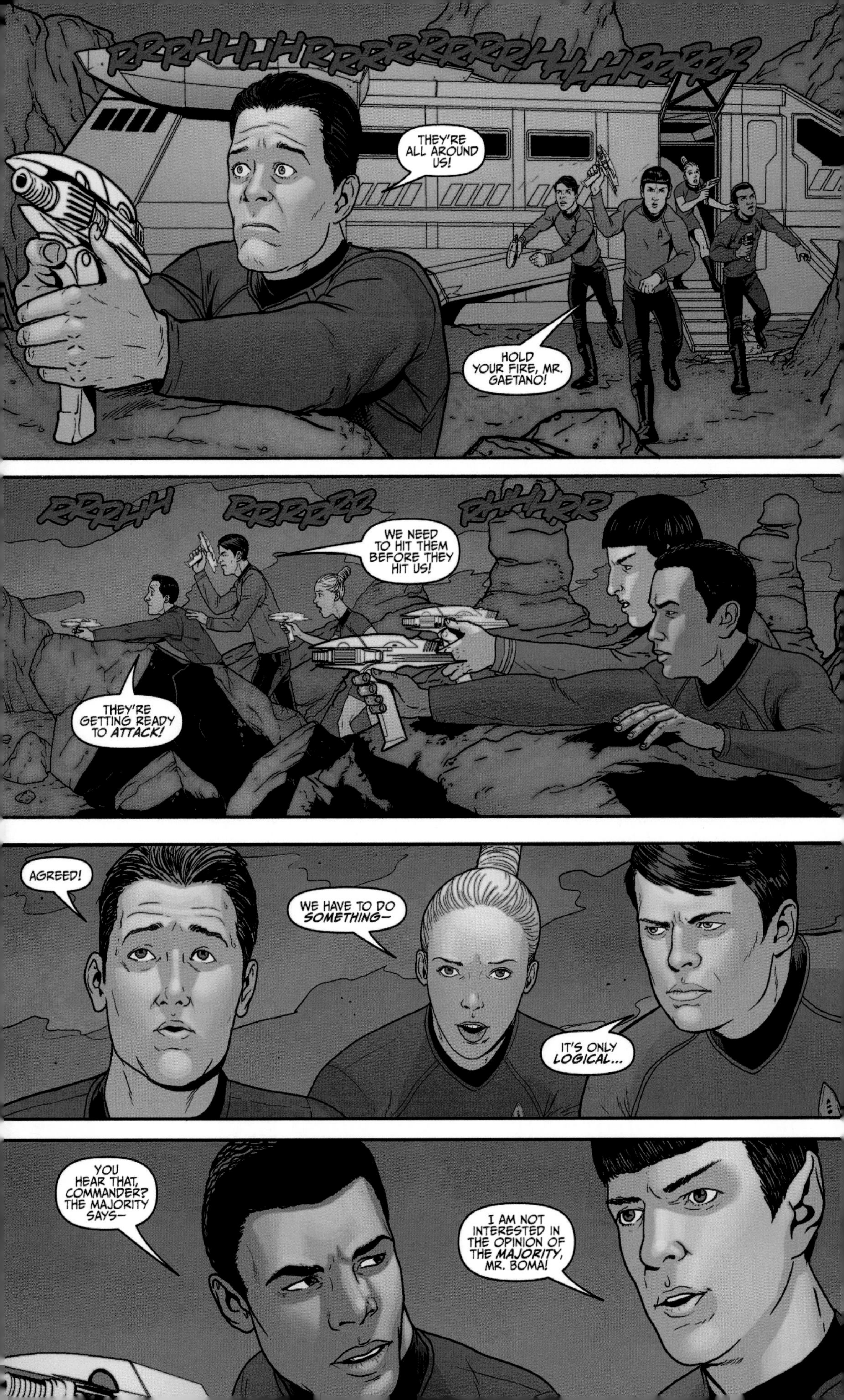
RRRHHHHRRRRRRRRRRHHHHRRRRRR
THEY'RE ALL AROUND US!
HOLD YOUR FIRE, MR. GAETANO!
RRRHH
RRRRRRR
RHHHRR
WE NEED TO HIT THEM BEFORE THEY HIT US!
THEY'RE GETTING READY TO ATTACK!
AGREED!
WE HAVE TO DO SOMETHING—
IT'S ONLY LOGICAL...
YOU HEAR THAT, COMMANDER? THE MAJORITY SAYS—
I AM NOT INTERESTED IN THE OPINION OF THE MAJORITY, MR. BOMA!

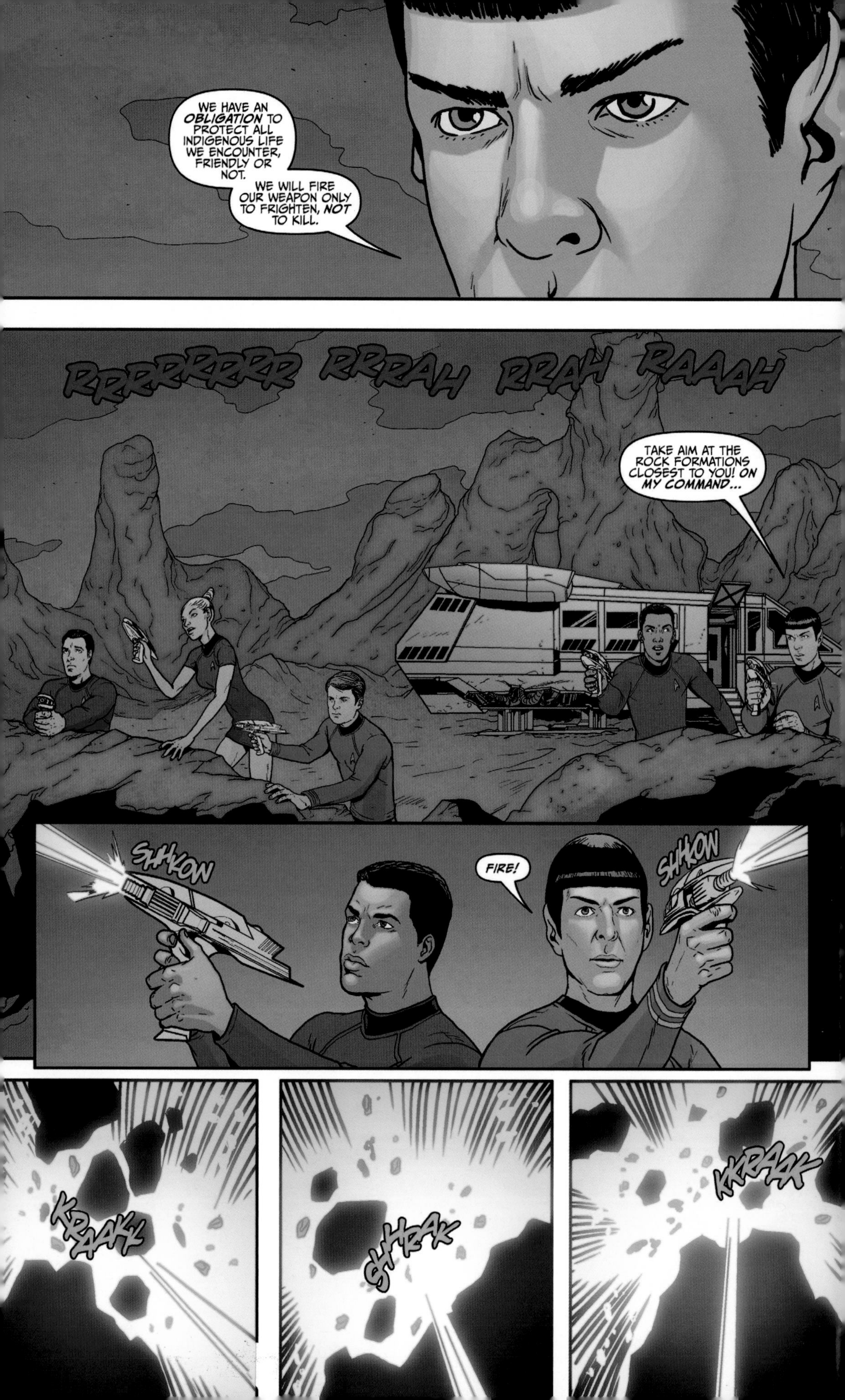
WE HAVE AN OBLIGATION TO PROTECT ALL INDIGENOUS LIFE WE ENCOUNTER, FRIENDLY OR NOT.
WE WILL FIRE OUR WEAPON ONLY TO FRIGHTEN, NOT TO KILL.
RRRRRRRR RRRAH RRAH RAAAH
TAKE AIM AT THE ROCK FORMATIONS CLOSEST TO YOU! ON MY COMMAND...
SHHKOW
FIRE!
SHHKOW
KRAAKK
SHHRAK
KKRAAK

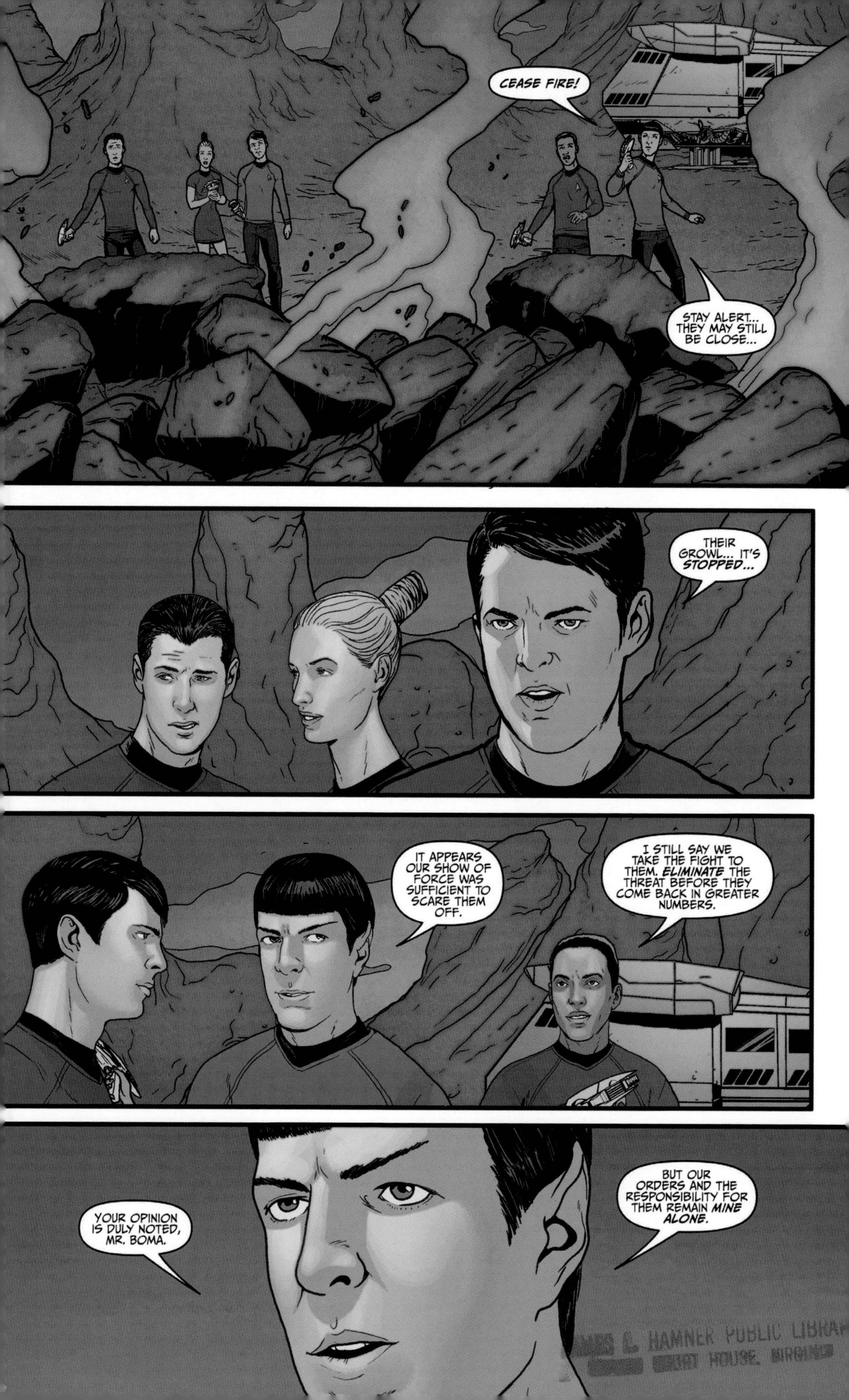
CEASE FIRE!
STAY ALERT... THEY MAY STILL BE CLOSE...
THEIR GROWL... IT'S *STOPPED*...
IT APPEARS OUR SHOW OF FORCE WAS SUFFICIENT TO SCARE THEM OFF.
I STILL SAY WE TAKE THE FIGHT TO THEM. *ELIMINATE* THE THREAT BEFORE THEY COME BACK IN GREATER NUMBERS.
YOUR OPINION IS DULY NOTED, MR. BOMA.
BUT OUR ORDERS AND THE RESPONSIBILITY FOR THEM REMAIN *MINE ALONE*.

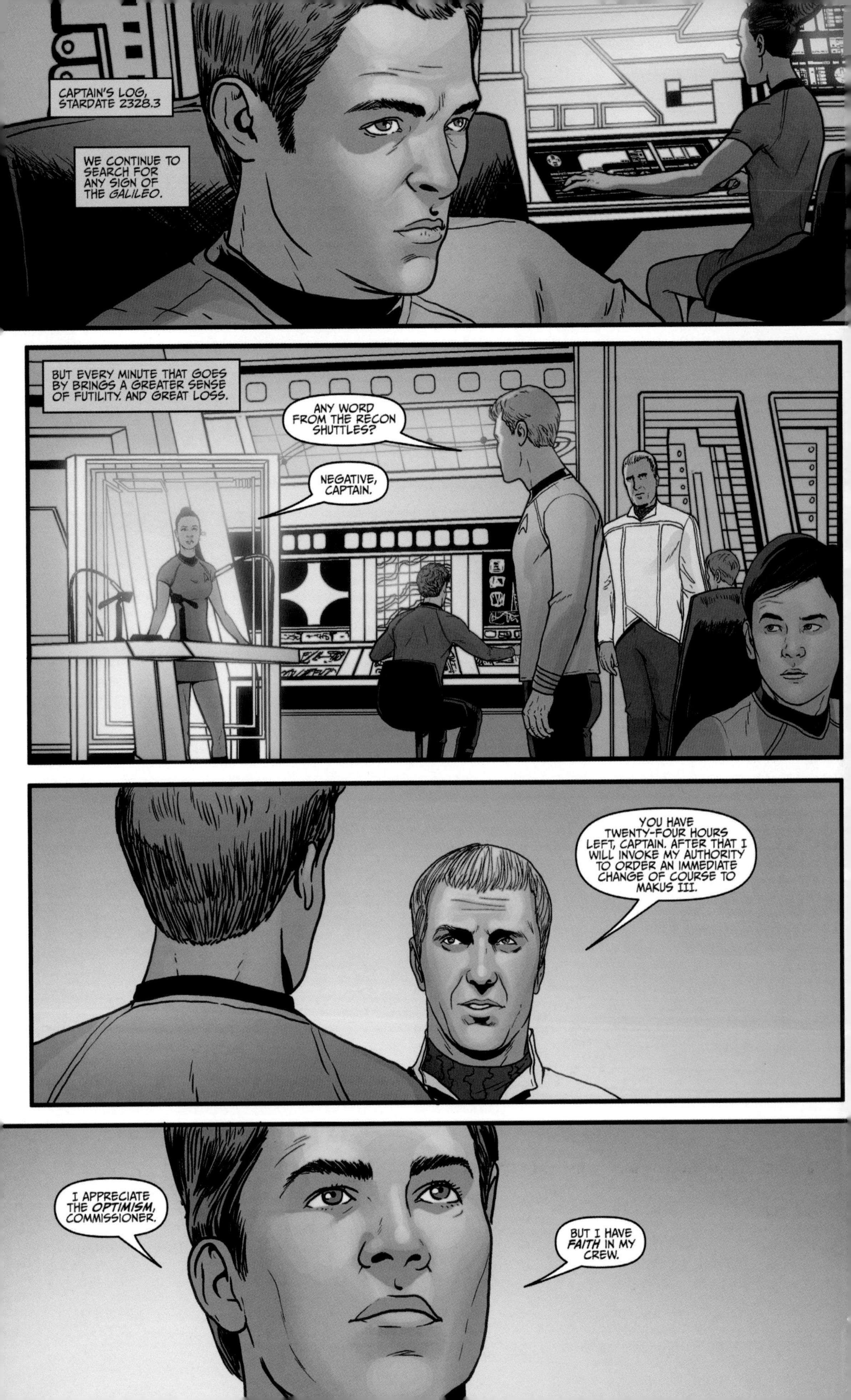
CAPTAIN'S LOG, STARDATE 2328.3
WE CONTINUE TO SEARCH FOR ANY SIGN OF THE *GALILEO*.
BUT EVERY MINUTE THAT GOES BY BRINGS A GREATER SENSE OF FUTILITY. AND GREAT LOSS.
ANY WORD FROM THE RECON SHUTTLES?
NEGATIVE, CAPTAIN.
YOU HAVE TWENTY-FOUR HOURS LEFT, CAPTAIN. AFTER THAT I WILL INVOKE MY AUTHORITY TO ORDER AN IMMEDIATE CHANGE OF COURSE TO MAKUS III.
I APPRECIATE THE *OPTIMISM*, COMMISSIONER.
BUT I HAVE *FAITH* IN MY CREW.

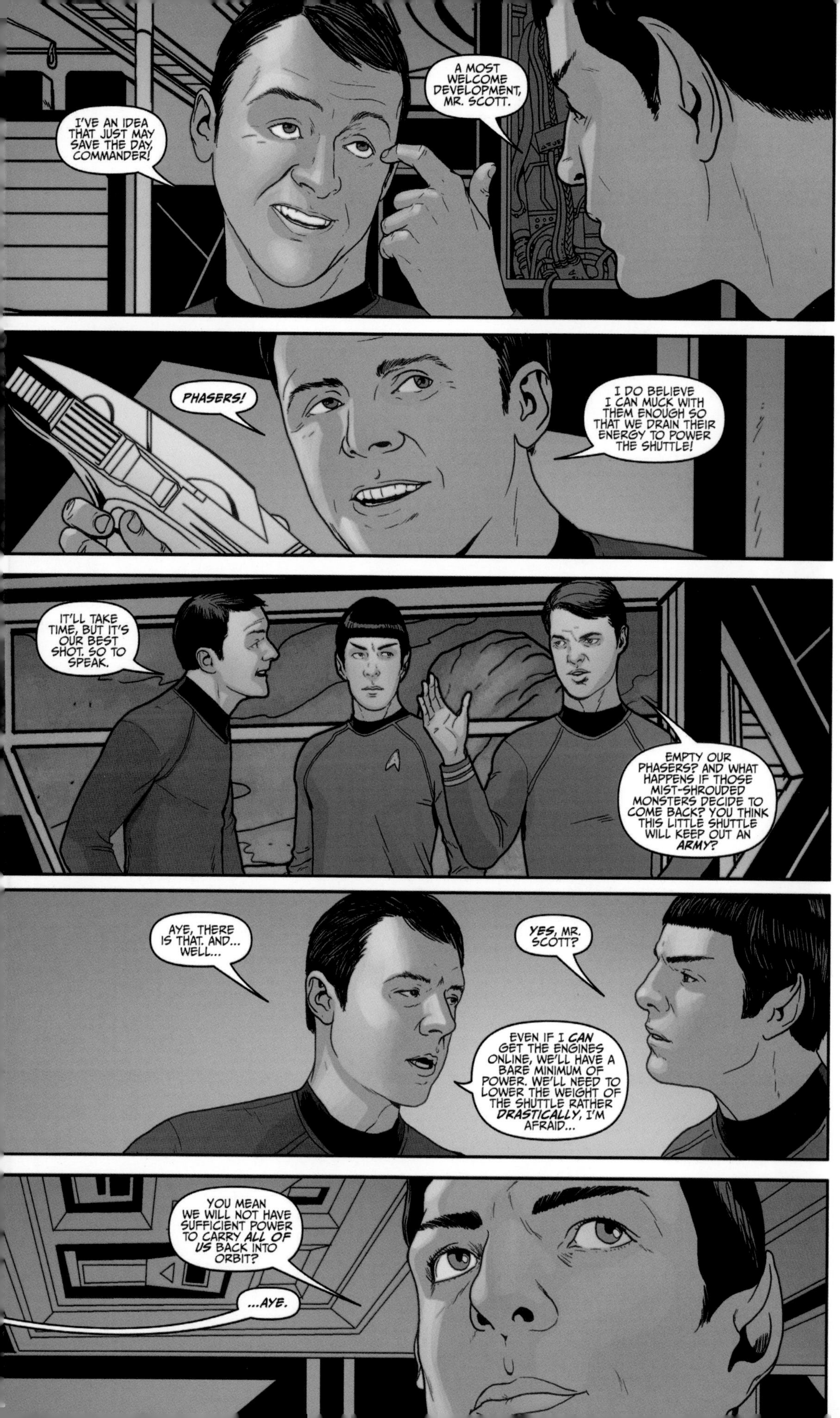
I'VE AN IDEA THAT JUST MAY SAVE THE DAY, COMMANDER!
A MOST WELCOME DEVELOPMENT, MR. SCOTT.
PHASERS!
I DO BELIEVE I CAN MUCK WITH THEM ENOUGH SO THAT WE DRAIN THEIR ENERGY TO POWER THE SHUTTLE!
IT'LL TAKE TIME, BUT IT'S OUR BEST SHOT. SO TO SPEAK.
EMPTY OUR PHASERS? AND WHAT HAPPENS IF THOSE MIST-SHROUDED MONSTERS DECIDE TO COME BACK? YOU THINK THIS LITTLE SHUTTLE WILL KEEP OUT AN ARMY?
AYE, THERE IS THAT. AND... WELL...
YES, MR. SCOTT?
EVEN IF I CAN GET THE ENGINES ONLINE, WE'LL HAVE A BARE MINIMUM OF POWER. WE'LL NEED TO LOWER THE WEIGHT OF THE SHUTTLE RATHER DRASTICALLY, I'M AFRAID...
YOU MEAN WE WILL NOT HAVE SUFFICIENT POWER TO CARRY ALL OF US BACK INTO ORBIT?
...AYE.

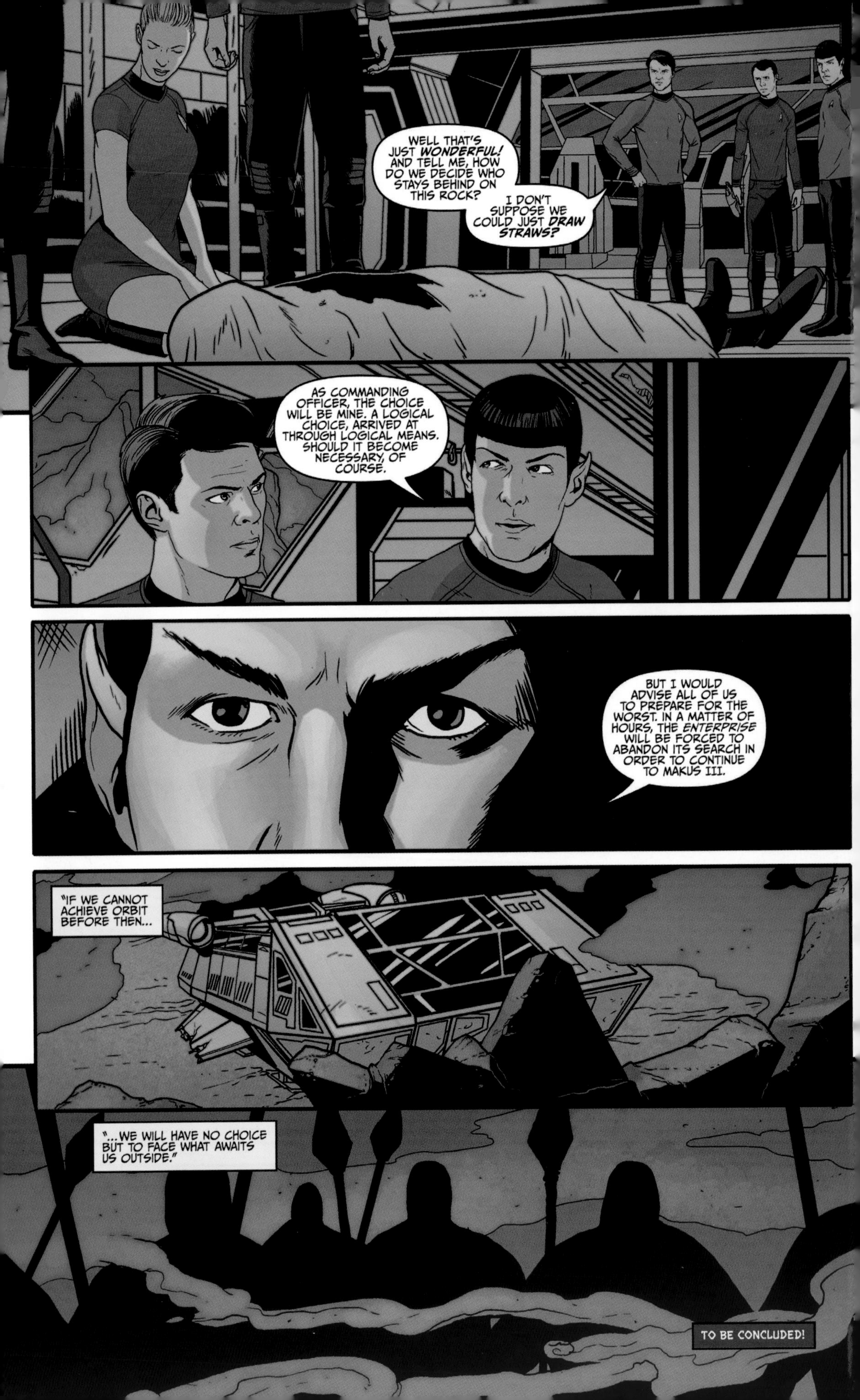
WELL THAT'S JUST WONDERFUL! AND TELL ME, HOW DO WE DECIDE WHO STAYS BEHIND ON THIS ROCK?
I DON'T SUPPOSE WE COULD JUST DRAW STRAWS?
AS COMMANDING OFFICER, THE CHOICE WILL BE MINE. A LOGICAL CHOICE, ARRIVED AT THROUGH LOGICAL MEANS. SHOULD IT BECOME NECESSARY, OF COURSE.
BUT I WOULD ADVISE ALL OF US TO PREPARE FOR THE WORST. IN A MATTER OF HOURS, THE ENTERPRISE WILL BE FORCED TO ABANDON ITS SEARCH IN ORDER TO CONTINUE TO MAKUS III.
"IF WE CANNOT ACHIEVE ORBIT BEFORE THEN...
"...WE WILL HAVE NO CHOICE BUT TO FACE WHAT AWAITS US OUTSIDE."
TO BE CONCLUDED!